A Drop of Gold

Written and Illustrated by

Vlasta van Kampen

Annick Press

Toronto • New York • Vancouver

©2001 Vlasta van Kampen (text and illustrations)
Cover design: Sheryl Shapiro

Annick Press Ltd.

We acknowledge the support of the Canada Council for the Arts, the Ontario Arts
Council, and the Government of Canada through the Book Publishing Industry
Development Program (BPIDP) for our publishing activities.

Cataloging in Publication Data

Van Kampen, Vlasta
  A drop of gold

ISBN 1-55037-677-2 (bound)   ISBN 1-55037-676-4 (pbk.)

I. Title.

PS8593.A56D76 2001   jC813'.54   C2001-930091-3
PZ7.V326 Dr 2001

The art in this book was rendered in watercolors.
The text was typeset in Charlotte Sans.

Distributed in Canada by: Published in the U.S.A. by Annick Press (U.S.) Ltd.
Firefly Books Ltd.   Distributed in the U.S.A. by:
3680 Victoria Park Avenue   Firefly Books (U.S.) Inc.
Willowdale, ON   P.O. Box 1338
M2H 3K1   Ellicott Station
                                   Buffalo, NY 14205

Printed and bound by Kromar Printing, Winnipeg, Manitoba.

visit us at: www.annickpress.com

For my dad, who builds birdhouses that keep the swallows returning to my garden every spring. —VvK

The world was new and full of color—

except for the birds. Mother Nature had been so busy making everything beautiful that she had forgotten the birds. They were still white and looked very much alike.

Mother Nature heard their sad chirping.

She knew she must make them beautiful too.

She gathered all the birds together.

Then she called her helpers, who came with pails of paint, lots and lots of brushes, and an overflowing basket of supplies.

The birds lined up and the monkeys started painting.

They painted and painted, adding stripes, specks, and spots, until almost no paint was left.

Legs and necks were stretched.

A few birds

wanted fancy feathers.

Some tried on new
feet and combs,

unusual beaks, bills,

and masks.

One big bill was left over. It was shaped
like a boat and its bottom could stretch.

A wise bird decided it would be perfect for fishing.

When all the decorating was finished,

the birds danced and whirled around, showing off their fine new feathers, feet, beaks, masks, combs, and colors.

Above the heads of the dancing birds, a tiny white bird fluttered about, chirping loudly. The dancing stopped.

"I got lost on my way here. Sorry I'm late," the little bird peeped. "I want to be painted blue, with lovely orange dots on my chest."

When the monkeys told him there was only
brown paint left, the tiny bird started to cry.

The monkeys chattered. The birds chirped.
They couldn't think of anything! And so the
little bird was painted brown.

The little bird looked down at himself.

"But I am so plain and you are all so beautiful. I have no specks, stripes, or fancy feathers," he said sadly.

Duck remembered the tiny pot that was
only to be used for something special.

They hadn't used it yet, duck reminded monkey. He grinned as he handed it to her.

A drop of gold fell from duck's wing into the little bird's throat. He shook his head, chirped, then began to sing.

Everyone listened. The little bird was still plain brown. He had no fancy specks or stripes. Instead, he had a golden voice, a voice like no other.

One day his name would be Nightingale.